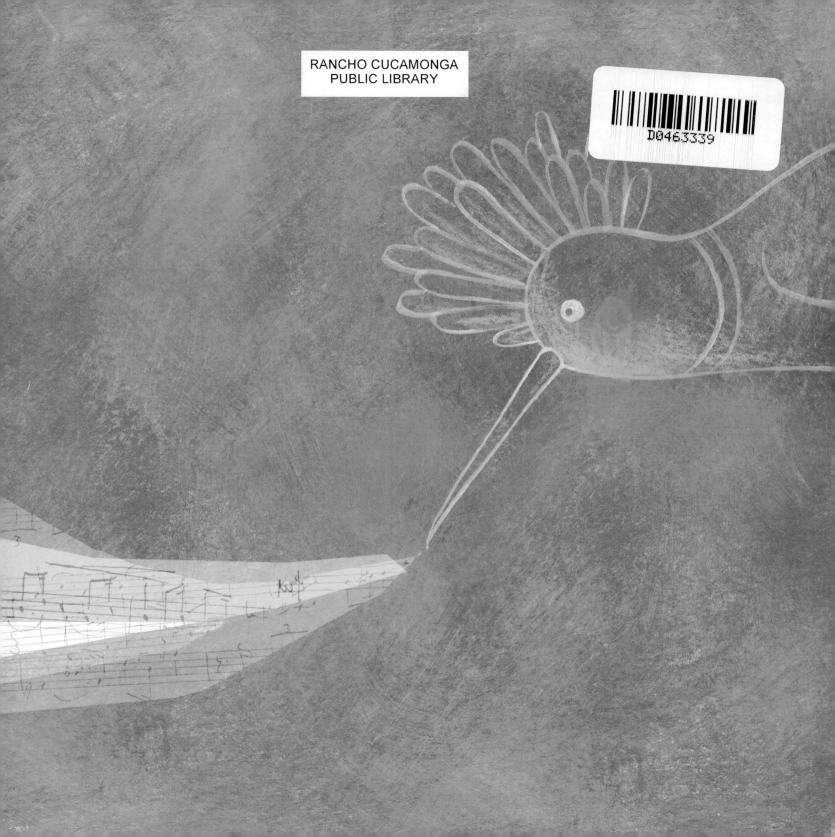

Lili Ferreirós & Sonja Wimmer

John's Whistle

CUENTO
DE LUZ

To all the Johns in the world who teach us to how to decipher the
language of love with all of its mysterious and powerful meaning.

- Lili Ferreirós -

To my mother, who can whistle better than anyone.

- Sonja Wimmer -

John's Whistle

Text © Lili Ferreirós
Illustrations © Sonja Wimmer
This edition © 2013 Cuento de Luz SL
Calle Claveles 10 | Urb Monteclaro | Pozuelo de Alarcón | 28223 | Madrid | Spain
www.cuentodeluz.com
Original title in Spanish: El silbido de Juan
English translation by Jon Brokenbrow

ISBN: 978-84-15784-12-8

Printed by Shanghai Chenxi Printing Co., Ltd. March 2013, print number 1355-4

FSC
www.fsc.org
MIX
Paper from
responsible sources
FSC® C007923

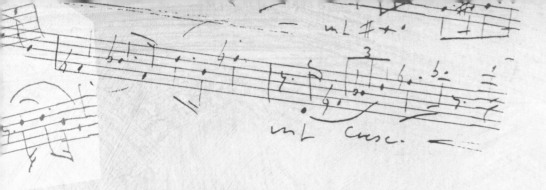

John had whistled since he was little. In fact, his first word wasn't a word at all. It was a whistle.

His grandparents, his aunts and uncles and his closest neighbors said that it was something that had been in his family for a long, long time. One of his ancestors had been famous for his way of whistling.

The problem was that when John was at the age when other children begin to speak, John didn't. And as he grew up, whenever he wanted to ask for something or express how he felt, he could only whistle.

Time passed, and John's whistles began to develop into different sounds. He eventually had enough to fill a dictionary of unique sounds! A sharp whistle called people's attention, a louder whistle signaled that he was hungry, and an even louder one escaped when he was frightened. John blew short whistles when he was sad, and long, sweet whistles when he was happy. He blew a gentle, playful little whistle when he wanted to say "I love you," and a deeper, more serious sounding whistle when he wanted to say just the opposite.

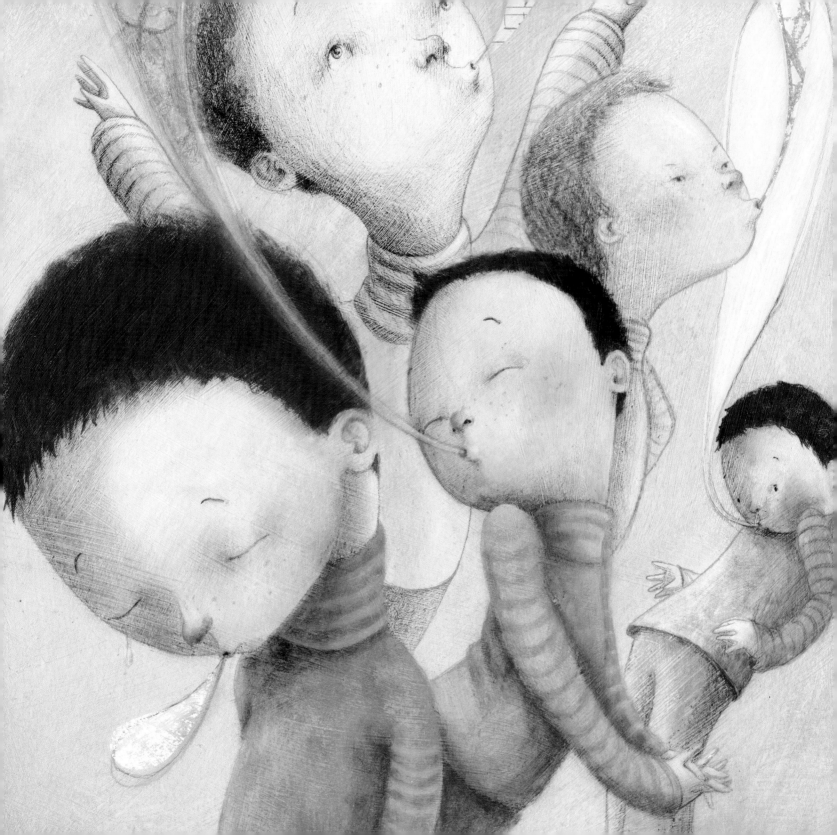

From the moment John began to whistle,
a gazillion birds flocked to his street,
his garden and even into his house! His
exasperated mother tried to chase them
off with her broom, but the birds just kept
coming back! Each one had its own song
with its own meaning, much like John's
whistle. Sometimes they seemed to be
talking to each other, and other times
they would blend their voices into a
breathtaking a cappella symphony.

But the grown-ups in the village didn't see
it this way, and they soon got fed up with
so much noise. But not the children: they
loved it and wished they could
sing and whistle, too.

It was easy to see (or hear!) why the children wanted to whistle like John. Even when the wind blew down in strong gusts from the top of the mountain and wove between the cottonwoods, it was possible to hear John's whistle from far, far away. His whistle had a power all its own, it was as simple as that.

But as wonderful as everyone else thought his whistle was, John's mother and father were anxious for him to learn to read and write. Although they worried that he may be at a disadvantage because he didn't speak like the other kids, they knew he had to go to school.

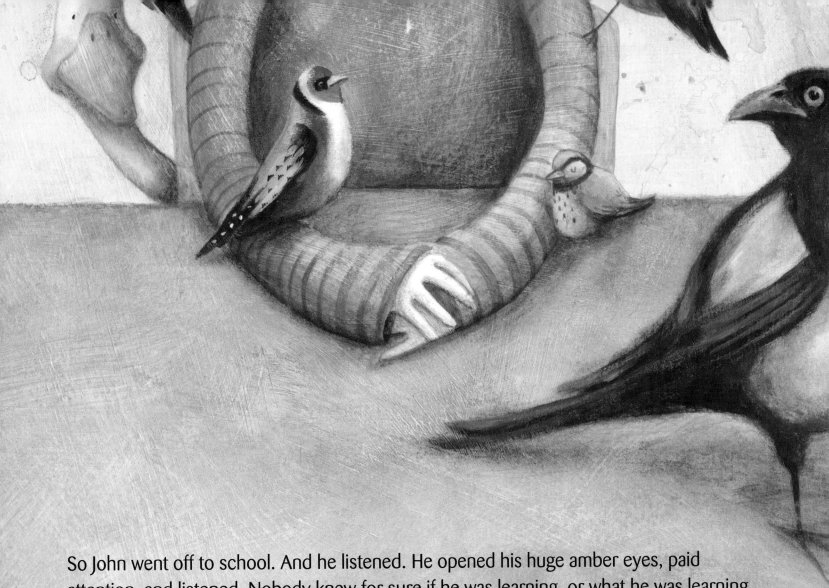

So John went off to school. And he listened. He opened his huge amber eyes, paid attention, and listened. Nobody knew for sure if he was learning, or what he was learning. But he listened and listened, more carefully than anyone else.

When the school nurse heard about John's whistle, she took him to the most distinguished specialists in the city. And what happened? Nothing. His inability to speak remained an absolute mystery. Even his teachers were captivated by his innocent expression and the incredible way he had of associating a whistle with each new thing he learned.

If they were learning about a river, John thought about where it began, how long it was, where it went, and where it entered the sea. And then he heard its voice, the voice of that river, and he told its story as only he could: by whistling.

If they were learning about trees, John would picture the way the branches moved in his mind and his whistling would accompany their graceful dance.

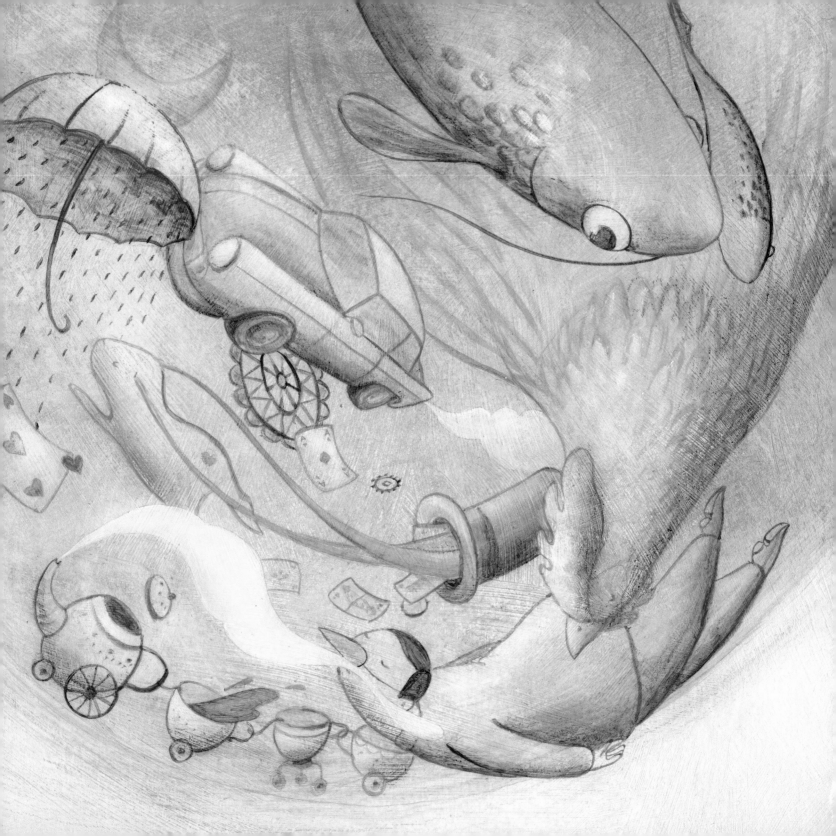

If they were learning about triangles, John would draw the shapes in the air with long whistles and silent pauses. With poems and stories, he was incredible! His whistles were like echoes that could move listeners to tears or laughter.

As the teachers saw that John enjoyed learning, and that his whistles actually helped the other kids rather than distract them, they allowed him to stay in the classroom.

John's friend Taleb didn't go to John's school, so he was surprised to see him sitting in the corridor with his dad one afternoon. He was even more surprised when he found out that Taleb would now be going to John's school, they would be in the same class, and that they would sit at the same desk!

At first, Taleb didn't talk either. But he was very good at drawing. Looking at Taleb's beautiful sketches, John could see the way the desert glimmered in the sun, how pretty Taleb's house was, how many brothers he had, and how much he loved olives.

They became quite the unique team! Because of course, John loved music, and he discovered that Taleb had another hidden talent as well…

Just how John discovered this was all thanks to their teacher, who, one day, told the class where Taleb was from, how a drought had forced him to leave his home, and that Taleb was amazing at playing the bendir. John had no idea what a bendir was, but Taleb demonstrated by tapping his hands on the table, gently at first and gradually playing faster and louder. That was when John's whistle filled the air. Soaring and leaping in time to the rhythm, it invited everyone to clap and dance.

The class turned into a party like it always did when John whistled.

And so, John and Taleb became
inseparable—in their music, and
in their friendship.

Until the day John discovered
that Taleb had feelings for Claire,
the girl with eyes as dark as night
who had caught John's eye.

When Taleb realized this, he
stopped drawing immediately.
John was upset with his friend,
but he knew Taleb meant no harm.

One Saturday morning, Claire and John bumped into each other on the street. Claire asked him to go with her into the woods on the mountainside to look for a bag of chestnuts. John felt as if a spring of mountain water was washing over his face. And, nervously at first, they set off.

When large rocks blocked their path, John would stretch out his hand and help Claire clamber over them. When there were thistles, he stretched his arm gently around her waist and helped her avoid them.

The sun blazed away, high in the sky, getting hotter and hotter. So they dove into the shade of the woods like fish into a lake, and once they had cooled down a little, they began to play hide-and-go-seek among the trees. For the first time on the whole trek, they burst out laughing.

Then Claire wanted to hide further into the woods.
"I wonder if she's behind that tree?" thought John.
She wasn't.
"Or that one?"
No luck.
"Or maybe that one over there?"
Still no luck.

Spinning around on his heels, he tried to call Claire with the special whistle he'd created just for her. But he couldn't. How strange! Where was his whistle? What had happened to it?

John began to run around, becoming more and more frightened. Was Claire in danger? Was she lost? He stopped abruptly. He tried to whistle again. Nothing. His lips had decided that they wouldn't do what he wanted them to do.

"¡CLAAAAiiRRRe!" he shouted with every ounce of strength in his body. "Claire!" he shouted again, amazed at how wonderful his own voice sounded. "¡CLAIRE!CLAire!"

Suddenly, he heard the crunching of dry leaves. Then, while he was listening, something unexpected, something miraculous happened.

John suddenly felt an unfamiliar storm rising in his throat…

From behind a majestic chestnut tree, Claire ran towards John and hugged him as hard as she could for a very long time.

Then, their eyes met, and they were never separated again.

The bag of chestnuts was forgotten, but John's whistle wasn't.

People say it didn't disappear completely. They say that from time to time, people ask him to do his magic; that each time he whistles, they can still see birds flying in the sky; and that he whistles while Taleb plays the bendir, and they make beautiful music together again in the village square.